D1631924

Previously published as:
My First Book of Fairy Tales
by Tiger Books International in 1989
My First Book of Bedtime Stories
by Tiger Books International in 1989

This edition published in 2010 by Chancellor Press,
an imprint of Octopus Publishing Group Ltd

An Hachette UK Company
www.hachette.co.uk

Reprinted 2011

Copyright © 2005 Octopus Publishing Group Ltd

All rights reserved. No part of this work may be reproduced or utilized in any form
or by any means, electronic or mechanical, including photocopying, recording or
by any information storage and retrieval system, without the prior written
permission of the publisher.

ISBN: 978-0-753720-48-6

A CIP catalogue record for this book is available from the British Library

Printed and bound in China

My first book of...
Fairy Tales & Bedtime Stories

CHANCELLOR
PRESS

CONTENTS

CONTENTS

LITTLE RED RIDING HOOD

One day, Little Red Riding Hood set out through the forest to visit her grandmother, who was ill. On the way, she met a large wolf.

Now the wolf was hungry, but he couldn't eat the girl because there were woodcutters nearby. So he asked her where she was going.

Little Red Riding Hood explained about her grandmother and told the wolf where the old lady lived.

The cunning wolf ran off to grandmother's cottage and gobbled up the old lady in a flash. Then he put on her nightdress and cap and jumped into bed, waiting for Little Red Riding Hood.

At last, she knocked on the door and the wolf said: "Come in."

"Goodness Granny," said Little Red Riding Hood as she went inside, "you must be ill,

your voice sounds so strange."

She went across to the bed to kiss her grandmother.

"Goodness Granny, what rough hairy arms you have!"

"All the better to hug you with, my dear," said the wolf.

"Goodness Granny, what big ears you have!"

"All the better to hear you with, my dear," replied the wolf.

"Goodness Granny, what huge teeth you have!"

"All the better to gobble you up with!" snarled the wolf springing out of bed.

Little Red Riding Hood ran for her life. One of the woodcutters heard her screams and rushed to her rescue. Down came his axe on the hairy head and the wolf lay dead on the ground. Little Red Riding Hood was saved, but you can be sure that she never talked to strangers again.

CINDERELLA

Once upon a time, there lived a girl called Cinderella, whose life was made wretched by her stepsisters. They made her into their servant; she had to cook and clean, wash and iron and wait on them hand and foot. In return, they pinched and slapped her and were never pleased with anything she did.

One day, a royal invitation arrived asking the sisters to the King's ball. There was great excitement: the house bustled all day long with dressmakers, jewellers, hairdressers, and dancing masters.

At last, the sisters were ready and swept off without even thanking Cinderella for all her hard work.

Cinderella sank exhausted onto her stool by the fire. "I wish I could go to the ball," she said and a tear slipped down her face.

"You shall go to the ball!" exclaimed a voice.

Cinderella looked up and saw a little old lady.

"I am your Fairy Godmother, do as I say quickly and your wish will come true."

Cinderella did as she was told. She fetched a pumpkin from the garden, mice from the cellar and lizards from the flowerpots.

Her Fairy Godmother waved her magic wand and they turned into a golden coach with six horses and footmen.

Cinderella's ragged dress became a ball-gown embroidered with jewels and her bare feet were in glass slippers that shone like diamonds.

"Go," said the Godmother, "but leave before the clock strikes midnight or the spell will end."

Cinderella was the success of the ball. The Prince fell in love with the beautiful and

mysterious young woman. Cinderella forgot the time, midnight struck and she tore herself from the Prince's arms. As she ran home, she lost a glass slipper on the palace stairs.

The Prince found the slipper, but not Cinderella. He travelled the Kingdom searching for his lost love. He tried the glass slipper on the foot of every woman, including Cinderella's cruel sisters, but it fitted no one.

In despair, he cried: "Is there no one else here?"

"There's me," said Cinderella. Her sisters pushed her away, but the Prince asked Cinderella to try on the slipper. It fitted perfectly. Cinderella married the Prince and they lived happily ever after.

THE UGLY DUCKLING

Once upon a time, a duck hatched six of the prettiest yellow, fluffy ducklings ever seen. But the seventh duckling, which hatched from a huge egg, was the ugliest duckling on the farm. It was big and grey and from the start everyone disliked it.

His own brothers and sisters kept saying: "If only the cat would get you, you hideous object!"

His own mother wished him far away and the hens pecked him.

He was so unhappy that he ran away. As he flew, he scared the little birds in the bushes. "It's because I'm so ugly," sighed the duckling and a tear rolled down his beak. He met the wild ducks.

"Gosh," they quacked, "you're ugly." Everywhere he went it was the same and

the ugly duckling became more and more miserable.

Winter came, it was bitterly cold. The duckling had to keep swimming to prevent his pond from freezing altogether. At last he grew faint, lay quite still and froze fast in the ice.

Early in the morning, a farmer found him. He broke the ice and took him home to the warm farmhouse kitchen where the duckling revived.

The children wanted to play with the duckling, but he thought they meant to hurt him so he flew around the room. He crashed into the milk can, upset the butter and knocked the flour to the floor. The farmer's wife chased him. Luckily the door was open and he escaped.

When spring arrived, the ugly duckling could not face life any more. One day, he saw three beautiful swans on a lake.

"I will fly towards the royal birds and they

will peck me to death because I am so ugly."

So he flew out on to the water until the swans saw him and rushed towards him. He closed his eyes and waited for death.

Instead, the swans swam round him making friendly noises. The duckling asked them why.

"You are one of us," they replied. "Look at yourself."

So he opened his eyes and saw his reflection in the water. A magnificent white swan looked back at him. He was no longer the ugly duckling and all the other swans bowed to him.

BEAUTY AND THE BEAST

Once upon a time, there lived a girl who was as beautiful as she was good. Her father called her Beauty and he loved her very much. One day he had to go on a long journey, but he promised to bring Beauty back a rose.

The merchant travelled all day and by nightfall he was quite lost. Stumbling through a wood, he went down an overgrown path. At the end he found a castle; the door was open so the merchant went inside where a servant gave him food and a soft bed for the night.

In the morning, the merchant looked for the master of the house to thank him. He entered a glorious rose garden and picked a rose for Beauty. As he cut the stem, there was a great roar. Terrified, the merchant fell to the ground.

A huge, hairy hand pulled him to his feet; a creature with the head of a monster and the shape of a human roared at him:

"Ungrateful man, why have you stolen my rose?"

The shaking merchant explained the gift for his daughter.

"I kill anyone who steals my roses," said the Beast, "but if you bring me your daughter, I will not kill you. Promise or die."

The merchant promised and went home.

Three months later, he returned and gave Beauty to the Beast. Beauty did her best to hide her fear, but the Beast was more hideous than she had imagined.

In spite of his looks, the Beast was kind to Beauty. One evening, watching her quietly, he said to her:

"Beauty, will you marry me?"

"No Beast," replied Beauty. The Beast gave a great sigh and his face crumpled with

sadness. After that he asked Beauty the question every night and her answer was always the same.

Although life with the Beast was not terrible, Beauty was homesick; she longed to see her father. She began to look miserable and ill and the Beast, afraid that she would die, agreed to let her go home for a month if she promised to return.

Beauty promised and went home to her father, who was overjoyed to see her.

Beauty forgot time. Two months passed, then she dreamed about the Beast. He was thin and mournful and looked as if he was about to die. Beauty was filled with remorse at breaking her promise and rushed back to the castle. She found Beast lying in the rose garden.

"Beast!" she cried, "Please do not die, I will marry you twenty times if only you will not die." She flung her arms around his neck

and kissed him.

At that instant the garden was filled with light and music. Beauty looked at the Beast in astonishment: he had changed into a handsome young prince who gazed at her lovingly.

"Thank you Beauty," said the prince. "Your unselfish love has broken the spell of a wicked fairy and I am myself. Now will you marry me?"

I expect you can guess Beauty's answer.

SNOW WHITE

Once upon a time there lived a very vain Queen. She gazed at herself in mirrors all day. One of the mirrors was magical and when the Queen looked in it she said:

"Mirror, mirror on the wall,
Who is the fairest one of all?"

The mirror replied:

"Beautiful Queen, so proud and tall,
You are the fairest one of all."

One day, the Queen asked the mirror her usual question and the mirror replied:

"Beautiful Queen, so proud and tall,
Snow White is the fairest one of all."

The Queen flew into a terrible rage. Princess Snow White was her step-daughter and the Queen was already very jealous of her. She commanded her huntsman to take Snow White into the forest and kill her.

The huntsman obeyed, but when he came to kill Snow White, he pitied her and set her free. So Snow White wandered through the trees and found a little house. She was so tired that, when there was no reply to her knocking, she let herself in and lay down on a little bed and fell asleep.

When she woke she was surrounded by dwarfs! "Who are you?" they asked kindly. Snow White told them her story and they decided that she must stay with them. Snow White happily agreed.

Far away in the palace the Queen asked the mirror who was now the most beautiful. It replied:

"Beautiful Queen, so proud and tall,
You were once the fairest of all,
But Snow White lives with the dwarfs so
  small
And she is the fairest one of all."

The Queen was furious that Snow White was still alive, so she disguised herself as a pedlar woman and travelled to the dwarfs' house. When the pedlar woman knocked on the door, Snow White bought some ribbons for her bodice.

"Let me help you lace them properly," said the wicked Queen and she pulled them tighter and tighter until Snow White could not breathe and fell as if dead.

When the dwarfs came home they cut the ribbons and Snow White revived. The dwarfs told Snow White never to let anyone into the house again.

Meanwhile the Queen spoke to her mirror

again, but the mirror said:

"Beautiful Queen, so proud and tall,
Snow White is the fairest one of all."

This time the Queen shook with rage.
"Snow White shall die," she cried. She
poured poison into one half of a rosy apple.
She found Snow White in the garden of the
dwarfs' house. "Take this red apple as a
present, my dear," said the evil woman.
"Oh I mustn't," said Snow White.
"I will cut it in half and eat it with you,"
said the wily Queen. So Snow White bit into
her half of the apple and fell dead at the
Queen's feet.
When the dwarfs found her they tried every
remedy, but they could not rouse her. At last,
they sorrowfully admitted that she was dead.
She looked so beautiful that they made her a
glass coffin and wrote in letters of gold on the

lid: "Snow White, a Royal Princess", placing it on a mountain.

A Prince came by and saw the glass coffin. He gazed at the beautiful Princess inside. The dwarfs told the Prince her sad story.

"I cannot live without looking at her," said the Prince. "Please let me take her with me."

At first the dwarfs refused, but in the end they were sorry for the Prince and agreed.

As the Prince's servants raised the coffin, one of them tripped and the jolt shook the piece of poisoned apple from Snow White's throat. She opened her eyes, and, sitting up, saw the Prince.

"I love you more than anything in the world," he said. "Please marry me." So she did. She rode away with her Prince, taking the dwarfs' wedding gift – a beautiful fawn.

When the wicked Queen heard about the wedding of Snow White, she burst her heart with rage and died.

GOLDILOCKS AND THE THREE BEARS

Once upon a time, there were three bears. There was a big bear, a middle-sized bear and a little, baby bear and they lived in a cottage in a wood.

One morning, the three bears made porridge for breakfast. It was too hot to eat, so they left it and went for a walk while it cooled down. A little girl called Goldilocks came wandering along and saw their pretty house.

She peeped in at the window and saw three steaming bowls of porridge.

"Mmmmm, they look good," she said and went inside.

She tried the porridge in the big bowl: it burnt her tongue. Then she tasted the porridge in the middle-sized bowl: it wasn't sweet enough. So she tried the porridge in the little bowl: it was just right, so she ate it all up.

Then she tried all the chairs; but Big Bear's chair was much too large, Middle-Sized Bear's chair was too hard, and Little Bear's chair was too small and she broke it.

By now she was feeling very tired, so she went upstairs and saw three beds. The big bed was too enormous, the middle-sized bed was too hard, and the little bed was just the right size, so she laid down and fell asleep.

The three bears came home to eat their porridge, but when they saw their bowls, Big Bear growled:

"Someone's been eating my porridge."

"Someone's been eating my porridge," said Middle-Sized Bear.

"Someone's been eating my porridge and has eaten it all up," said Little Bear.

They looked around and saw their chairs.

"Someone's been sitting in my chair," said Big Bear.

"Someone's been sitting in my chair," said

Middle-Sized Bear.

"Someone's been sitting in my chair and has broken it," cried Little Bear.

Then they went upstairs. "Someone's been sleeping in my bed," growled Big Bear.

"Someone's been sleeping in my bed," said Middle-Sized Bear.

"Someone's been sleeping in my bed and she's still there," squeaked Little Bear at the top of his voice.

The noise woke Goldilocks, who leapt out of bed in fright at seeing the three bears. She jumped out of the window and ran home as fast as her legs could carry her.

THE PRINCESS AND THE PEA

Once upon a stormy night, a princess knocked at a castle gate. At least, she said she was a princess, but all the Queen could see was a dripping girl with muddy shoes.

"We'll see," thought the Queen: she wanted a real princess to marry her son.

The Queen put a pea on the mattress of the guest bed. Then she piled twenty mattresses on top of the pea. That night the Princess slept on them all.

"How did you sleep?" asked the Queen in the morning.

"Very badly," said the Princess. "There was something hard under the mattresses. I tossed and turned all night and I'm black and blue this morning."

The Prince married her, for only a real Princess could have such delicate feeling.

JACK AND THE BEANSTALK

Once upon a time, a poor widow sent her son Jack to sell their only cow. On the way to market Jack met a butcher who gave him a bag of beans for the cow. Jack's mother was so angry with Jack when he arrived home that she threw the beans out of the window.

The next day, a huge beanstalk had grown beside the cottage. It was so big that the top disappeared into the clouds. It was too tempting for Jack, who climbed up it. When he got to the top he met a fairy.

"You must be Jack," said the fairy. "I know all about you." She told Jack how, many years before, his father had been killed by a giant who had taken all the family's riches.

Jack was determined to find the giant and punish him for his wickedness, so he set out

for the ogre's castle.

When he got there he slipped inside and hid. Soon the giant arrived home and in a voice of thunder called:

"Fee fi fo fum,
I smell the blood of an Englishman."

But although he searched everywhere he could not find Jack, so he shouted for his hen.

"Lay," roared the giant, and the hen laid a huge golden egg. She continued to lay, but the giant, tired after hunting all day, fell asleep.

Jack crept out of his hiding place and, snatching up the hen, ran to the top of the beanstalk and slithered down to his mother.

The hen laid many golden eggs for Jack, and soon he and his mother were rich. But Jack could not forget that the giant had killed his father and was determined to take his

revenge. So, once more, he climbed the beanstalk and hid in the giant's castle.

When the giant came home he roared,

"Fee fi fo fum,
  I CAN smell the blood of an Englishman.
When I catch you I'll eat you alive."

Jack jumped out of his hiding place and ran like mad for the beanstalk. The giant began to scramble down after him, but Jack landed first and, grabbing an axe, hacked at the beanstalk until it crashed to the ground, killing the giant instantly. Jack, his mother, and the hen lived happily together.

PUSS IN BOOTS

Once upon a time, a miller died and left nothing to his youngest son but a cat. The young man was miserable.

"I might as well skin you for a pair of gloves," he said to the cat. "You'd be more use to me dead than alive."

"Now that's just where you're wrong," said the cat. "I'd be more use to you alive than dead."

The young man was speechless with astonishment: the cat could talk.

The cat continued, "Dear master, give me a pair of leather boots and I will make you rich."

So the young man gave the cat a fine, little pair of leather boots and Puss set off to make his master's fortune.

First, Puss caught two big rabbits and

M.W. Tarrant

presented them to the King.

"A present for you, Sire, with the compliments of my master, the Marquis of Carabas."

The king was amused by the talking cat and thanked him.

When Puss heard that the King was out driving with his beautiful daughter, he bounded across the fields to the castle of an ogre telling his master to follow.

Puss rang the doorbell and, when the ogre answered, he bowed low and said that he had heard the ogre was a clever magician able to change himself into different animals.

The ogre was very vain and invited the cat into the castle to see his magic. He muttered a spell and became a huge lion.

Puss arched his back and bushed his tail but congratulated the ogre on his cleverness.

"Now how about a very small creature, such as a mouse?" suggested the cunning cat.

In a twinkling, the ogre became a tiny squeaking mouse and Puss gobbled him up.

When his master arrived, Puss dressed him in the ogre's fine clothes and together they waited for the King's coach. As it drove up, they bowed low.

The King said to his daughter, "Why, it's the talking cat I told you about, my dear."

"And this," said Puss, "is my master the Marquis of Carabas and his castle. We have prepared a feast for you."

After that, the Princess and the Marquis fell in love and were married. Puss was given a new pair of boots and led the wedding procession.

THE SLEEPING BEAUTY

Once upon a time, a King and Queen had a beautiful baby. All the fairies in the land were invited to the christening of the little Princess. All except one who was wicked.

At the christening, the fairies gave the baby Princess gifts of beauty, kindness, courage, and cleverness.

The ceremony had just finished when the wicked fairy flew in at the door.

"I'll teach you to leave me out," she hissed as she darted towards the cradle. "My gift to you little Princess, is that you will prick your finger on a spindle and die."

She flew away, her shrieks of laughter echoing through the palace.

The King and Queen were terrified, but the good fairies, although unable to stop the spell, promised that the Princess would not

die when she pricked her finger, but would fall asleep for a hundred years.

On her fifteenth birthday, the Princess played hide and seek. Looking for someone, she went into a turret where she had never been and saw an old woman spinning.

"What are you doing?" asked the Princess.

"Spinning, Your Highness," replied the old woman.

"May I try?" said the Princess. The old lady gave her the spindle.

Immediately, the Princess pricked her finger and fell into a deep sleep. The King laid her on her embroidered bed. The spell was very strong and soon the whole palace fell asleep. A thick hedge of thorns grew round and hid it. As years passed, no one could even remember where the palace had been.

One hundred years later, a prince was hunting in the forest when he saw the towers of a palace above the trees. He rode towards

them, but his way was barred by a thick thorn hedge. He cut a path through and found a huge doorway. Opening it, he entered the enchanted palace. Ignoring the sleeping figures all around him, he searched every room. Finally, he opened a door and found Sleeping Beauty.

The Prince kissed her and broke the spell. She woke and so did the whole palace. The Prince married the Princess and they lived happily ever after.

BEDTIME STORIES

MRS. BUN'S BIG WORRY

You know, don't you, that rabbits are timid creatures. You know that they are very easily frightened.

Well, Mrs. Bun is the most timid rabbit of them all. She is *always* fretting and worrying about something. She frets and worries so much, she frightens herself!

Mr. Bun is the opposite. He stays calm, no matter what. Each night Mrs. Bun stands in her nightgown and worries out loud, "What if burglars break in while we're asleep? What if the house catches on fire? What if it rains and the roof leaks?" But Mr. Bun just kisses her on her soft pink nose and says, "Sleep well."

One night, she woke him up at five o' clock in the morning. "Oh, Mr. Bun! I've had such a terrible dream! I must tell you!"

Mr. Bun opened one eye and lifted one ear off the pillow. "Tell me your dream then, dear," he said patiently.

"I dreamed, I dreamed – oh me! It was dreadful! I dreamed the children had to do my shopping for me!"

"That doesn't sound dreadful," said Mr. Bun. "That sounds like a great idea." But he went on listening with one sleepy ear.

"I gave them some money and I asked them to buy me an onion and some carrots, a spoon and some nuts, a cabbage and six fresh eggs . . ."

Now for those of you who don't know, Mr. and Mrs. Bun have two children. It's easy to tell them apart: Currant has a little fluffy brown tail, and Cream has a little fluffy white one. Everyone knows what good, helpful little rabbits they are; and Mrs. Bun often asks them to help her around the house, dusting and polishing.

In her dream Mrs. Bun gave them a basket to carry the groceries and told them, "You must be careful. Walk, don't run. And don't play so that you drop the basket and spill the groceries and break the eggs."

"We would *never* do that," said Currant.

"Never *ever* do that," promised his sister Cream.

Off they went, as good as gold. They found the shop and bought the groceries – an onion and some carrots, a spoon and some nuts, a cabbage and six fresh eggs. And they set off for home again, carrying the heavy basket between them.

Currant and Cream didn't play on the way home. No, no.
They walked – they didn't run. Certainly they didn't.

In fact they were as sensible as two small rabbits can be.

But suddenly . . .

A great big black-and-white puppy dog came into sight, bouncing and bounding and barking. Of course Currant and Cream were terrified!

Would the puppy see them?

Would he chase them?

Would he bite them?

Quick as a flash, the two young rabbits hid behind a tree. How their delicate whiskers trembled as the noise came closer and closer to where they were hiding!

Fortunately, the puppy went bouncing and bounding and barking by.

Currant popped out from behind the tree and cried, "Come on, Cream! Let's get out of here before he spots us!" And he grabbed the basket and took a great stride toward home, all the time looking over his shoulder, watching out for the puppy.

So of course he didn't see the knotty tree root sticking up out of the ground.

Down he tumbled and down went the basket, too. Out spilled the onion, the cabbage, and the spoon. Out spilled the carrots and the nuts. But worst of all, out spilled the eggs:

Cr-plack! Cr-plack! Cr-plack!

All six of them broke into one big yellow squelch.

"Oh dear! Oh dear!" cried silly Mrs. Bun tugging on her husband's ears in terror. "If I send Cream and Currant shopping, my dream is bound to come true!"

"Nonsense," said Mr. Bun, refolding his ears on his pillow. "Send Cream and Currant shopping as often as you like."

"But the eggs will all get broken!"

Mr. Bun sighed. "So send them to buy onions and cabbages, carrots and spoons and nuts. *Only leave out the eggs.* Then if the basket gets dropped, nothing will break at all. Now wake me up when it's morning. Night-night."

WHEELIE WINNIE

"What's this? What's this?" cried Scratch Squirrel. She was perched up at the top of the tall pine tree in the middle of the woods, collecting nuts for the winter. But the tree began to shake under her.

The high branches shook so much that Scratch dropped one of her nuts.

As the little squirrel peered down through the leaves she saw a man was swinging a long, heavy axe. With each blow he cut a big notch out of the tree's trunk.

"Hey! You can't do that!" cried Scratch. "Don't you know that this is the Extra Special Tree?"

"That's why the toymaker asked us to cut it down," replied the woodcutter. "He wants to make an extra special toy."

Several men tied ropes around the tree and heaved until the great forest pine gave a groan and fell to the ground.

They cut it into logs and carted them away to the toymaker's yard. There the toymaker picked up one piece of wood after another and looked them over carefully until he found one that was just right.

Then he sawed it and planed it, he shaped and carved and turned it, he whittled and sanded it, he polished and painted it. He took some wool and some horsehair and some leather, too, and he made a mane and a tail and a bridle. Can you guess what kind of toy he was making?

Of course! A horse!

Finally he nailed on four wheels and a handle for pushing and stood the horse in the window of his shop. On a sign he wrote
AN EXTRA SPECIAL HORSE
FOR AN EXTRA SPECIAL PERSON

Ronnie was that extra special person.

His mother and father bought the extra special toy for their extra special boy, and on the morning of his birthday Ronnie found the wooden horse standing by his chair at the breakfast table.

Oh, there never was such a birthday present! Ronnie had always wanted a horse of his own.

"Will she let me ride her? Will she gallop? Will she trot? Will she canter? Will she rear up and snort and snicker? Will she whinny?"

"That sounds like a name – Wheelie Winnie!" said his sister Jane, laughing. "You should call her Wheelie Winnie – because she has four wheels and horses whinny when they're happy!"

So that's what the horse was called. And Ronnie says he heard her softly whinnying that very night as if to say, "I'm very happy here in my new home."

Baby wanted to ride Winnie.

Of course, Ronnie had to say yes because children must always be ready to share their toys. But Baby's legs were too short to reach the ground when he sat astride, and he rolled off and bumped his head and cried. So he was not allowed to ride Winnie again.

Jane wanted to ride Winnie, too. But her legs were too long; they got in the way.

So only Ronnie could ride Wheelie Winnie, because he was just the right size. He was secretly pleased about that. So was Wheelie Winnie.

"We shall go on lots of adventures together and fight battles and explore dangerous places and race the wind," whispered Ronnie. He built Winnie a stable out of boxes beside his bed. As he dozed off to sleep, one hand resting on Winnie's woolen mane, he thought he felt the little horse nod and he heard her whinny with joy.

ELFRED THE DRAGON RIDER

It seemed like an ordinary day.

John only meant to go out for a ride in his toy car, then come home again for lunch. He only stopped beside the Old Oak Tree because it was such a hot day and the shade looked so cool. As he sat there, his back against the trunk, he watched the dragonflies dart to and fro through the tall grass.

When he saw him, he had to blink once and look again because he was such a very odd sight. But there he was! Astride one of the dragonflies sat a little elf, dressed in a green tunic and a pointy red hat. Everything about the elf was pointy – his sharp little nose, his sharp little ears, the toes of his boots. And he was pointing at John as if to say, "Giddyup, dragonfly! He's the one!"

The dragonfly landed right on John's knee, and off hopped the elf. "I'm Elfred the Dragon Rider. You look like a giant, so I'd better fight you and cut off your head!"

"I'm not a giant," said John quickly. "I'm only a little boy. And I don't want to fight you. I'd rather be friends."

"Whew. That's lucky!" exclaimed Elfred. "If we're going to be friends, you should come and visit my home. That's what friends do. Oh, but you'd better eat this first."

Elfred took a tiny red apple out of his pocket and gave it to John. At the first tiny bite John started to get smaller and smaller, until he was no bigger than Elfred himself. Then off they flew.

The elf's home was a tree house at the top of the Old Oak. Elfred and John had to climb up a rope ladder to reach it, but it was worth the effort because there were bowls of strawberries waiting for them.

"Delicious!" said John. "But I must be going soon, or people will start to worry. How do I get big again?"

"Oh dear," said Elfred. "I've never done that magic before. I don't know."

"Well, who does?" cried John. "I don't want to be this small forever!"

"Don't worry," said Elfred. "Let's visit Wizard Woops. He'll know the magic spell."

So they went to visit the old wizard, and he mixed a magic potion for them in a big cooking pot over the fire.

The magic potion tasted very nice – like bananas and honey – but it didn't make John big again.

"Oh dear," sighed Wizard Woops. "This *should* be as easy as flying. All you need is a special magic word from my Great Dictionary of Magic. But I'm afraid More-Gone the Pirate stole it. You will just have to go and find More-Gone and get the book back."

He took them outdoors, where the leaves looked as big as row boats to people as tiny as Elfred and John. The wizard sprinkled magic over two of the leaves, and at once they floated off the ground. "Climb in and hold tight!" said the wizard. "These chariots will take you wherever you want to go."

"Take us to More-Gone the Pirate!" cried Elfred, and their leaf-chariots carried them over hills and rivers, deserts and seas to where hot, sandy islands poked up out of a blue ocean. There, in the distance, lay the pirate galleon, and tied to the mast was a tiny yellow-haired prisoner – a beautiful girl elf.

Down they swooped between the sails and ropes to the deck of the galleon. The ship was deserted. All the pirates had gone ashore to bury their treasure. So John freed the pirate's prisoner (whose name was Elfleda) and she clambered aboard his leaf-chariot.

"To the beach!" cried John.

"Thank you for rescuing me!" whispered Elfleda in John's ear.

"You're welcome," said John. "Do you know where More-Gone has hidden the Great Dictionary he stole from Wizard Woops?"

"Oh, yes. It's in that treasure chest – the one they are burying in the sand now."

So Elfred and Elfleda and John simply waited until the pirates had gone, then dug up the treasure chest and found the book.

"Here's the magic word," said Elfred. "To get back to where you started, all you have to say is . . . but wait, you will come and visit us again, won't you?"

"Of course!" cried John.

"Heckleflecklepop," said Elfred.

"Excuse me?"

"That's the word. You just say –"

"Heckleflecklepop!" said John, and found himself sitting in the shade of the Old Oak, just as big (or as little) a boy as ever.

Margaret W. Tarrant

CURRANT, CREAM, AND EGGS

"I would really enjoy an egg for my dinner!" said Mr. Bun, forgetting how Mrs. Bun loved to worry.

"Oh dear, oh dear. But if I send Currant and Cream to the store, they might drop the eggs on the way home. Oh, the waste of money! Oh, the waste of eggs! Oh dear!"

"Never mind," said Mr. Bun sadly. "It really doesn't matter."

Currant, overhearing this, whispered to his sister, "Why don't we get Dad an egg for his dinner. Mrs. Hen might give us just one, if we ask nicely. Then Ma will see how we *can* carry eggs home safely without breaking them."

They had only got as far as the crossroads when they met Mrs. Hen. "Please would you give us one of your eggs as a surprise for our Dad?" asked Cream sweetly.

"I'll give you six eggs if you will help me look for my chicks!" wailed Mrs. Hen jumping from one foot to the other. "I just turned my back for a moment, and they wandered off! Now they are lost, lost, lost, and it will be dark soon. Then what will become of my poor little ones?"

"Don't worry," said Currant. "I'll take this road, Cream will take that road, and you can take the third. Between us we'll search until we find your lost chicks, Mrs. Hen."

They searched and they called; they called and they searched. But whenever Currant or Cream saw a fluffy speck of yellow in the grass, it popped out of sight before they could reach the spot.

"I think those naughty chicks are playing a game and hiding from us," said Cream to Currant.

"Well, I'll soon put a stop to that!" said her brother.

Currant coughed and said in a loud, loud voice, "Come along, Mrs. Hen. Come along, Cream! It's getting very dark and it is foolish to be outdoors after dark. There are *foxes* and *weasels* and *owls* and all sorts of *dangerous animals* out hunting for something small and delicious to eat. Hurry! Let's go home!"

And taking Mrs. Hen, one by each wing, they rushed her home, despite her loud, squawking protests.

As they went, though, Currant and Cream made very sure to flash their fluffy tails in the twilight so that the naughty little chicks could keep sight of them and follow on behind without getting lost.

In their hiding place in the tall grass, Pick and Peck looked at each other and shivered. "*Foxes!*" they exclaimed.

"*And weasels!*"

"*And owls!*"

"*And other dangerous animals!*"

When Currant and Cream got back to Mrs. Hen's house, they pretended to lock and bolt the door. "Home is the only safe place to be after dark!" said Cream in as loud a voice as she could manage.

No sooner had the two little rabbits sat down, then there came a desperate *knock, knock, knock*. In tumbled Pick and Peck. "Oh, Ma! Oh, Ma! We won't ever wander off again! Why, we might have been eaten up by *foxes* or *weasels* or *owls* or some other *dangerous animal!*"

Of course, Mrs. Hen tried to be cross, but she was just so happy to see her children again. Then she filled the basket with fresh eggs; it was so heavy that Currant and Cream had to carry it between them. "Hurry home now. It really *is* dangerous to be out after dark," said Mrs. Hen. "And be careful not to drop the basket." She did not understand why the two little rabbits giggled.

The little family of chickens stood on the steps to wave goodbye. But of course Currant and Cream could not wave back because they were carrying the eggs so very carefully.

"I wish I had a fluffy white tail like Cream," said Peck.

"I wish I had a fluffy brown tail like Currant," said Pick.

"When you are grownup, sensible chickens, you will both have great big tails like bright feathery fans," said their mother, ". . . but only if you keep away from *foxes* and *weasels* and *owls* and don't run off and hide in the tall grass."

I think the chicks learned their lesson.

But what do you think happened to that full basket of eggs? Did it reach home safely? Did Mr. Bun have his surprise dinner? Did Mrs. Bun stop worrying about sending Currant and Cream to the store to buy eggs? I do hope so.

THE GREAT RACE

One day Ronnie was out riding his wonderful wooden horse, Wheelie Winnie, when they met Scott, the boy who lived next door. Scott was riding a new, shiny red scooter, and how fast he went.

"*Vroom!*" roared Scott, and he charged right at Ronnie and banged into him. It might have frightened Winnie had she not been so very brave.

"Silly old donkey!" shrieked Scott. "You call that a horse? Why it's just a silly old wooden donkey!"

(Scott was not a very likeable boy.)

"She's not! She's the best horse in the whole world!" said Ronnie angrily.

"Prove it then," said Scott. "Let's have a race. Race you! Race you! Race you to the bottom of the hill! Or are you too scared?"

Now Ronnie could sort of feel through his knees that Wheelie Winnie did not like the idea. But Scott only sneered and jeered, "Scaredy-cat! Won't race! Doesn't dare!"

Well, that made Ronnie so mad he decided to do it.

They started the race right at the top of the hill. Ronnie tucked up his knees and Winnie rolled faster and faster on her round wooden wheels. But she was not as fast as Scott's scooter! He went hurtling down the hill too fast to stop!

At the bottom of the hill, Scott's scooter skidded one way, and he slid another. A moment later Wheelie Winnie crashed into the scooter and Ronnie went down too.

What a disaster! When Ronnie picked up his beloved horse, one wheel was off and all the paint was scraped on one side.

"Looks bad," said Mr. Baker, who had been watching the race.

Scott ran home crying, leaving his scooter in the road. Ronnie didn't cry. He was too worried about Wheelie Winnie.

But Mr. Baker, who had seen the accident, found a nail and took a big stone and banged the wheel back on. Then Ronnie wheeled his horse home very gently and took her to the shed. He found a can of paint and painted Winnie's stripes just as they had been before. He didn't tell anybody about the race or the accident until Wheelie Winnie was looking as good as new.

His mother told him he must *never* race down the hill; then she looked at the little wooden horse. "I'm glad that Winnie didn't hurt herself," she said " like that red scooter I saw all scraped and bent, lying in the road."

"I'm sorry, Winnie," whispered Ronnie in his horse's ear. And it seemed as if Winnie shook her head and said, "That's all right – just don't do it again!"

DRAGON WEDDING

One day John met his friend Elfred under the Old Oak. The little elf was bursting to tell him an exciting piece of news.

"The Sea Dragons are getting married! I heard it from the Mermaids – they're the first to know anything that happens in Fairyland. Everybody is invited! Would you like to come?"

"Absolutely!" cried John. So he ate one of the elf's magic red apples to make him as small as an elf himself. "Who will I meet at the wedding?" he asked.

"Oh, everyone who's anyone: the Seagulls, the Fairies, the Seahorse, the Penguins – the Mermaids of course – and every dragon you have ever seen, naturally."

"I've never seen any dragons before," said John. "Will Elfleda be there?"

"Never seen any dragons?" cried Elfred. "What have you been doing all these years?"

"Are they very terrifying?" asked John as they rode through the air in their leaf-chariots toward the forests of Fairyland.

"Dragons? Not terrifying at all if you like green and don't mind them having two heads each."

"But what can I give them as a wedding present?"

"Oh, no need for that. Things are different in Fairyland. At weddings there, all the guests get presents instead – one wish each. The King and Queen see to that."

John would have asked more questions, but the sound of music grew too loud below them. They had arrived at the dragon wedding.

And what a wedding! It was sunset before the happy couple spread their four wings, nodded their four heads to thank everybody and flew away on their honeymoon.

Only after they had gone did the King and Queen of the Fairies arrive with a train of a thousand fairies. The King and Queen had shining butterfly wings of purple and white, and they wore golden crowns on their heads.

"They come later so the guests aren't distracted from watching the bride and groom," whispered Elfred. John could understand that – although he thought Elfleda was prettier than anyone there.

Soon the King summoned John to his throne. "We have heard much about you," he said. "How you rescued Elfleda from the Pirates and returned the Great Dictionary to Wizard Woops. Kneel down and I will dub you a Knight of the Order of Elves!"

So John knelt down as a little boy and rose as a Knight-Elf. In his excitement he almost forgot the magic word – *Heckleflecklepop* – that would take him out of Fairyland and back home again.

MR. BUN'S PIPE

"Oh dear, oh dear. I do worry about Mr. Bun smoking that old pipe of his. I'm sure it isn't good for him," thought Mrs. Bun one day. (You know how she loves to worry.) So when Mr. Bun put down his pipe, she hid it out of sight under the table.

Soon after, the family sat down to dinner, and Mrs. Bun bustled about in the kitchen, mumbling and muttering, "Oh I do hope the food hasn't burned. I do hope it's hot enough. I do hope I didn't use salt instead of sugar."

Then little Currant wrinkled his nose and started to sniff. "I smell a funny smell," he whispered to his sister.

Cream sniffed. "I smell it too," she said.

The two little rabbits peeped under the table, and what do you think they saw?

A curl of smoke and a lick of flame. "I don't like to worry you, Mother," said Cream gently, "but the carpet seems to be on fire."

"Oh my paws! Oh my ears! Oh my whiskers!" cried Mrs. Bun, turning as white as her tail. "It's all my fault! I hid the pipe! I've set fire to the house! I've burned down the very roof over our heads! We'll lose everything! We'll all die! And it's my fault! Oh, what a foolish rabbit I've been!"

While Mrs. Bun hopped about the room in confusion, Currant got a pitcher of water from the kitchen and put out the fire. "Well done, son," said Mr. Bun softly.

"Nothing to worry about," said Currant.

When they had finally persuaded Mrs. Bun to sit down and have a cup of tea, she promised she would never again hide Mr. Bun's pipe without asking him. "In fact," she said, "I'll never worry or fret ever again. It's far too dangerous!"

WINNIE TO THE RESCUE

Ronnie was glad when the rain stopped. For days and days it had been too wet to play outdoors, and he wanted very much to take Wheelie Winnie for a gallop in the park. Jane came too.

The ground was still very wet. The grass was muddy, and the path was spread with big round puddles. "Look over there!" exclaimed Jane. "That puddle is almost as big as a pond. And what's that in the middle of it?"

Crouched on a large rock in the middle of the puddle was a small black kitten. What a sad sort of a sound she was making, too!

Mew! Mew! Mew!

You see, the puddle had grown big around her, and she couldn't get to the edge. You know how kittens hate water! "Winnie will rescue her!" cried Ronnie.

He pushed Wheelie Winnie as far into the puddle as his arm would reach. The frightened kitten jumped upon Winnie's back, and Ronnie was able to pull her to the edge.

But oh! That little cat's claws dug sharply into Winnie's wooden back. And that water was so cold creeping around Winnie's wheels. There was a chance that the nails holding the wheels in place might go rusty, and then how would Winnie trot about?

"You are very brave!" said Ronnie hugging her painted neck. He saw her wet wheels and he rubbed off every last drop of water with a soft cloth, so that Winnie was as shiny as new.

"See how nice you look after your brave rescue!" said Ronnie, and he showed the little wooden horse her own reflection in a mirror.

And she had to admit, she did look somehow different.